To Kelly
From Josiah Johnson
Christmas 1995

A Michael Neugebauer Book
Copyright © 1987 Neugebauer Press Publishing Ltd. London.
Text by Lilian McCrea, with kind permission of Nursery World.
Published in USA by Picture Book Studio Ltd., Saxonville, MA.
Distributed in Canada by Vanwell Publishing, St. Catharines.
Published in U.K. by Neugebauer Press Publishing Ltd., London.
Distributed by Ragged Bears, Andover, England.
Distributed in Australia by Era Publications Ltd., Adelaide.
All rights reserved. Printed in Hong Kong.
LIBRARY OF CONGRESS CATALOGING IN PUBLICATION DATA
McCrea, Lilian
Mother Hen
Summary: Despite invitations from the other farm animals
to come out into the barnyard, Mother Hen stays on her nest
keeping her eggs warm.
[1. Chickens—Fiction. 2. Domestic animals — Fiction]
I. Reinl, Edda, ill. II. Title.
PZ7.M138184Mo 1987 [E] 86-25453
ISBN 0-88708-037-5

Ask your bookseller for this other Picture Book Studio book
by Edda Reinl:
THE THREE LITTLE PIGS

Lilian McCrea

Mother
Edda Reinl **Hen**

PICTURE BOOK STUDIO

Mother Hen was not out in the farmyard.
Where could she be?

Mother Hen was sitting on her nest in a corner of the barn. She had made her nest on top of a pile of soft, golden hay, and underneath Mother Hen were ten white eggs! Mother Hen was sitting on her ten white eggs to keep them warm.

Every morning the farmer came into the barn carrying a dish of corn and a basin of water. And he put them down on the floor just beside Mother Hen's nest.

"Now, Mother Hen," he said, "you haven't far to go for your breakfast!"

"Cluck, cluck. Thank you!" said Mother Hen, and she flew off her nest and pecked up the corn, and drank a little water. And in just a minute she was back again in her warm, soft nest sitting on her ten white eggs.

And every day Winkie, the farmer's brown-and-white cat, came softly into the barn on her four white feet, and said, "Mew, mew. It's sunny and warm in the farmyard today. Aren't you coming out, Mother Hen?"

But "Cluck, cluck," said Mother Hen. "I can't come out. I must sit on my eggs and keep them warm."

And she fluffed out her feathers and settled herself again on her nest of soft, golden hay where she cuddled her ten white eggs.

And every day Bob, the farmer's big furry dog, came into the barn, pit-pat on his four furry feet and said, "Bow-wow. It's a fine day for a walk. Aren't you coming out, Mother Hen?" But "Cluck, cluck," said Mother Hen. "I can't come out. I must sit on my eggs and keep them warm." And she fluffed out her feathers and settled herself again on her nest of soft, golden hay, where she cuddled her ten white eggs.

And when Strawberry, the farmer's red-and-white cow, came into the barn to be milked, she said, "Moo-oo. The grass in the fields is juicy and green. Aren't you coming out, Mother Hen?" But "Cluck, cluck," said Mother Hen. "I can't come out. I must sit on my eggs and keep them warm." And she fluffed out her feathers, and settled herself again on her nest of soft, golden hay, where she cuddled her ten white eggs.

And at night-time when Nobby, the farmer's big white horse, came into the barn to sleep, he said, "Neigh-eigh-eigh. You haven't been out all day, Mother Hen!" "Cluck, cluck," said Mother Hen, "I couldn't come out today, and I can't come out tomorrow. I must sit on my eggs and keep them warm." And she fluffed out her feathers and settled herself again on her nest of soft, golden hay, where she cuddled her ten white eggs.

Mother Hen sat on her nest of soft, golden hay and cuddled her ten white eggs for a very long time. Days and days went by, but still she sat on her nest.

Then one day Mother Hen heard a little noise underneath her that went *crick! crack!...* What do you think had happened?

A little yellow chicken had pecked open its white egg and come out from inside! "Cluck! cluck!" said Mother Hen. And just as she said that, *crick! crack!* went another white egg and out came another little yellow chicken! And *crick! crack!* went another! and another! and another! until all Mother Hen's white eggs were broken, and in her nest were ten yellow chickens!

"Cluck!, cluck. Come under my wings," said Mother Hen, and she spread her big red wings over her baby chickens. And "Peep, peep," they said, as they cuddled close to her warm, red, feathery body.

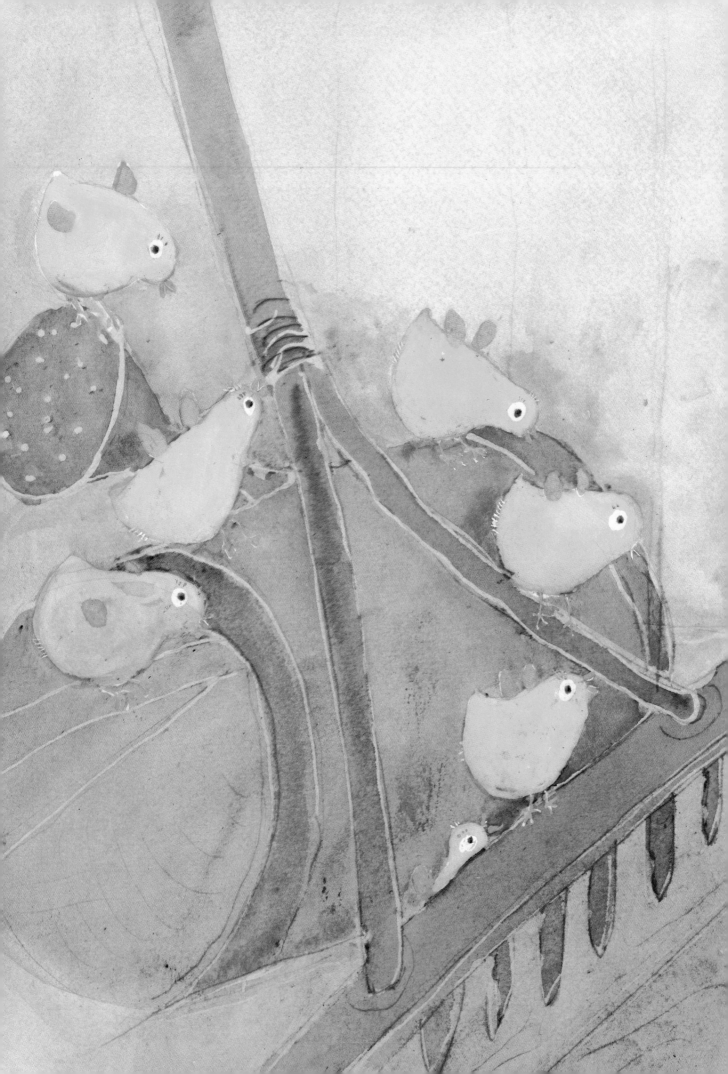

Then, in a little while, Mother Hen said, "Cluck, cluck! Come along now. The sun is shining, so we'll go for a walk." And Mother Hen got down off her nest, and her ten baby chickens came after her, calling, "Peep, peep. We're coming."

Out into the sunny farmyard went Mother Hen, with her ten baby chickens behind her. Winkie, the farmer's brown-and-white cat, was sitting in the sun washing her face. But when Mother Hen came along she stopped… and looked…

"Mew! mew!" she said. "Are those your yellow chickens, Mother Hen?"

"Cluck, cluck. All mine." said Mother Hen.

"Where did they come from?" asked Winkie.

"Cluck, cluck. They were inside my white eggs," said Mother Hen. "That's why I had to be so careful to keep my eggs nice and warm."

"Mew, mew. I must go and tell Bob," said Winkie.
And away she ran on her four white feet to Bob,
the farmer's big furry dog. "Mew, mew," she said.
"Do you know, Mother Hen has ten baby chickens
all her own!"
"Bow, wow!" said Bob. "I must go and tell Strawberry."

And off he ran on his four furry feet to Strawberry, the farmer's red-and-white cow. "Bow-wow," he said. "Do you know, Mother Hen has ten baby chickens all her own!"
"Moo-oo," said Strawberry. "I must tell Nobby."
"Moo-oo," she said to Nobby, the farmer's big white horse. "Do you know, Mother Hen has ten baby chickens all her own!"
"Neigh-eigh-eigh!" said Nobby. "Let's go and see!"

And Winkie and Bob and Strawberry and Nobby all went to the farmyard and there, walking about in the sunlight, was Mother Hen with her ten yellow chickens behind her. "Mew, mew," said Winkie. "Bow-wow," said Bob. "Moo-oo," said Strawberry. "Neigh-eigh-eigh," said Nobby.
"We like your yellow chickens, Mother Hen." "Cluck, cluck," said Mother Hen. "Thank you. Now we must go and find the farmer. He'll want to meet my yellow chickens, too." And off she went, with her ten baby chickens behind her, calling, "Peep, peep, here we come."